The MAGNIFICENT MUMMIES

Tony Bradman   Martin Chatterton

Banana Books

Far away in the Land of Sand . . .
. . . there flows a big, slow river.

(Who's that swimming in it?
Oh, never mind.)

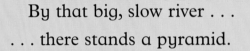

By that big, slow river . . .
. . . there stands a pyramid.

(Who's that putting up a sign?
Oh, never mind.)

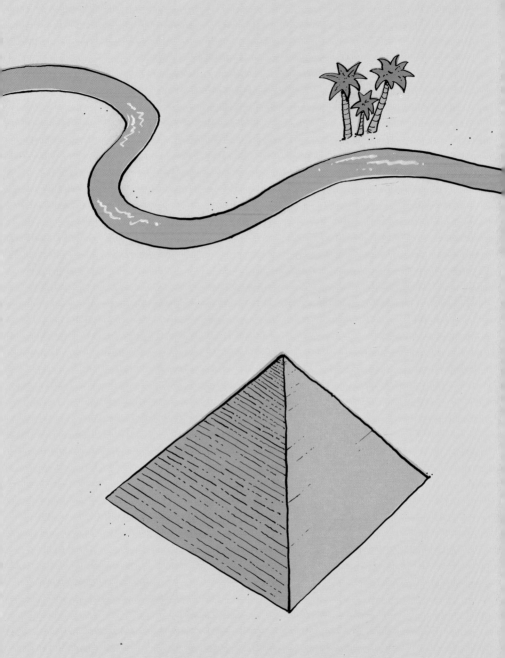

And inside that pyramid you'll find . . .

. . . a family of mummies.

And here they are to say hello!

The Mummies were having a quiet, restful day. Mummy Mummy was reading the paper. Daddy Mummy was cooking in the kitchen. And the Mummy kids were watching TV.

The Mummy family sat down at the table.
Tut and Sis were soon in trouble.

They were saved by a loud knocking noise!
The knocking went on, and on, and on.
So the Mummies went to the front door.

Daddy Mummy opened the door and the
Mummies peered out.

A man was standing outside.

The man didn't say anything. He just went
very pale ... and fainted dead away.

They brought him in, and brought him round. The man soon got over his surprise.

His name was Sir Digby Digger. He was an archaeologist, so he did lots of digging.

The Mummies asked Sir Digby to stay to tea. They laughed and joked and became great friends.

But at last it was time for Sir Digby to go.

The Mummies gave Sir Digby some old
things they didn't need any more.

He seemed quite pleased.
Then they took him to the
front door.

Sir Digby climbed into his car . . . but he didn't get very far.

His car made an odd coughing noise.

Sir Digby's car just wouldn't start!

Sir Digby lost his temper.

Sir Digby kicked his car, very hard.

The Mummy family and Sir Digby tried to
mend the car. But it was no use.
All it did was cough, cough, cough.
Sir Digby was rather upset.
He had an important appointment
at a monument in Memphis.
'It's at eight, and I mustn't
be late!' said Sir Digby.
Then Mummy Mummy had a
brilliant idea. She remembered
something she had seen in
the paper . . . and now
she led the way.

Bags I be . . .
the mechanic!

They all went round the corner, and there was the place Mummy Mummy had seen:

> The Two Sheikhs –
> Used Camels for Sale.

The Two Sheikhs were called Rattle and Roll and they were very helpful.

Sir Digby chose a camel and paid for it.

The camel left quite quickly.

The Mummies
waved goodbye.

'What shall we
do now?'

'The washing,
I think. You need
some clean
bandages!' said
Mummy Mummy.

So they collected
the dirty washing
and headed for the
river. But when they
arrived, they couldn't
believe their eyes.

The river had
vanished.

What a surprise!
The Mummies
were stumped.

They stood on the sand of the river bank
and looked down at more ... sand.

The Mummies set off to investigate.

I'm going to find the river!

Hey, wait for me!

Let me tell them!

No, I want to!

Tut and Sis ran ahead.
But they soon came
racing back.

Stop arguing, you two!

What have you found?

Tut and Sis were both very excited.
They dragged Mummy Mummy
and Daddy Mummy along
by the hands.

And there it was . . .
The BIGGEST creature they had ever seen.

It was a huge whale, and his name
was Moby.

He had got lost, and swum into the river by
mistake. Now he was stuck fast where the river
had started to grow narrow . . .

. . . and none of the water could flow past.

Poor Moby looked very unhappy.

Then Daddy Mummy
had a brilliant idea!

They needed someone who was good
at digging!
And they knew just the man for the job!

Daddy Mummy sent Tut and Sis dashing
to the Used Camel Lot with a message.

Minutes later a cloud of dust left the
pyramid.

Inside it were the Two Sheikhs.

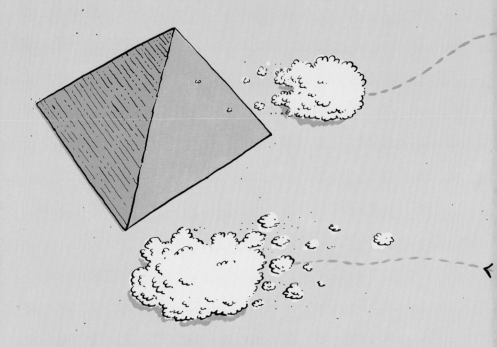

Soon a slightly bigger cloud of dust
returned. Inside that were the Two Sheikhs . . .
. . . and Sir Digby Digger!

But Sir Digby was a man with a plan.
He drew some lines in the sand . . . and got
everybody digging and digging and digging.

The river came flooding back. And
now there was a great big pool of lovely
cool water, too. Moby was free!

He was very pleased.

So he made sure that Sir Digby and the
Two Sheikhs and the Mummies had a
whale of a time!

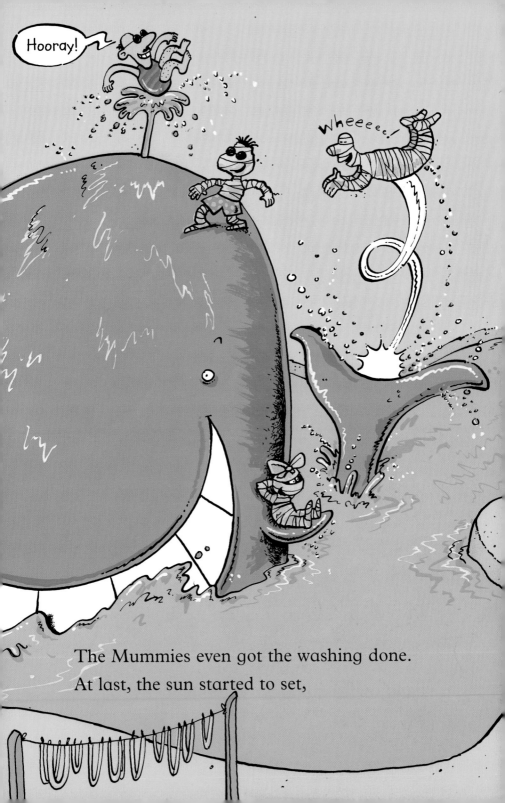

The Mummies even got the washing done.
At last, the sun started to set,

and it was time to go.

Sir Digby went . . .

the Two Sheikhs went . . .

Moby went . . .

and the Mummy family went as well.

On the way home, they were so happy, they
did the famous Mummy sand dance by the
light of the moon. It had been a wonderful day
in the Land of Sand.

And now the Mummies were very tired.

And that's the end of the story.

See you all
again soon!

Published specially for World Book Day 2004
First published in Great Britain 1997
by Egmont Books Ltd
239 Kensington High Street, London W8 6SA
Text copyright © Tony Bradman 1997
Illustrations copyright © Martin Chatterton 1997
The author and illustrator have asserted their moral rights.
Paperback ISBN 1 4052 1024 9
10 9 8 7 6 5 4 3 2 1
A CIP catalogue record for this title is available from the British Library.
Printed in U.A.E.